SHOWSTOPPER

RAE ELLIS

THE WHUMPY PRINTING PRESS

To the flu. The fever dream you granted me spawned the original 11,000 words of this story, which I wrote over the span of one delirious week. I'll never forget you <3

CONTENTS

— · —

Content Warnings

This story contains the following content:

- Serial Killer

- Yandere

- Snuff films

- Heavy violence, including knives, gore, and dismemberment

- Murder

- Nonconsensual drugging

- Taunting about a loved one's death

- Character death

If this book isn't for you, no worries! But if it is, we hope you enjoy this story about a detective and his suspect...

1

SHOWOFF

"Hey, *Shah* – "

Darian's head tipped up toward Amelia's voice, but his eyes didn't follow – too focused on following the steadily-blurring string of words that pillared down the too-bright screen of his laptop. "Yyyyyyyeah – ?" Half-distracted by the whirlwind of thoughts.

A file plopped onto his desk – thin, bulking in one spot.

He dragged his eyes from his work to it. "What's this?"

Amelia tapped at it. "Showoff's at it again."

Aaaaaaaaaand Darian's thoughts skittered to a stop, draining away almost noisily in his mind until only the file remained. "When did we get this?" He opened it, immediately plucking up the flash drive and plugging it into his laptop.

"Few minutes ago – east side this time. The guy gets around."

"Still don't know it's a guy, Amy. Check the language before you bias the team."

He could feel her eyes boring into him as he opened the file on his laptop, pulling up the MP4. "Just get the analysis in by this afternoon."

"Mhmm – " His voice was distracted again as he connected his earbuds and hit play. He didn't watch her leave.

He was already immersed.

'Showoff' was an entirely accurate name for this particular fucker. Out of all the serial killers he'd analyzed and tracked down, this one was easily the most elegant. Most just ... slashed and hit. So many killers pulled from trauma and took it out on their victims in explosions of violence.

Not this one. They were incredibly refined. Almost loving as they carved off piece after piece. They floated across the screen clad in thick black fabric, a simple craft store mask over their face.

For all intents and purposes, they appeared at a glance like any highschooler egging a house during homecoming week.

They didn't speak.

They didn't leave messages.

They didn't make demands or taunt their captive.

It wasn't until they moved that their beauty shone. Delicate as a butterfly's wings and elegant as a flower unfurling at first light. Every flick of the knife cut through Darian's heart like the gentlest Mary Oliver poem. Ecstasy dripped through him as the blood flowed from flesh, drawn out and strewn on display.

A linen cloth draped behind the pair – Showoff and the poor victim. A man this time. Shirt cut cleanly off. Gagged with a simple black cloth tied around his head. Not to keep him quiet – just to keep him from speaking.

The screams rang through all the same, muffled or not.

Darian kept his composure as he watched, keeping his face solemn and blank as he took notes. Notes on Showoff's height – it was easier to tell in this video – perhaps five foot eight. Dominant hand – left. Physical features ... still none. They covered themself too well.

Yet, the bulk of the clothes did nothing to hide the elegance of their movements. Their arm still floated through the air. Their body still glided across the ground. Darian couldn't see their legs shifting at the bottom of the screen, but they caught Show's form as easily as breathing, leaving no impact point. No rise and fall of their body. No upset in their gait.

Just gliding smooth as water. Smooth as always.

The knife traced and twirled in a dance around the captive's throat, leaving no mark there, only drawing out panting whimpers and muffled pleas as his head wrenched to the side, tucking against his shoulder to escape it.

Darian forced himself to pause the video and look away. Take a note on nothing – just the precision of the blade.

His best guess so far was that Show was an artist or doctor. Few others had that level of precision. And, wives' tale may it be, left-handers always seemed to fall more neatly into those occupations.

Darian focused on his breath. It was shaking again – he needed to get it under control before someone else on the team noticed. This office space offered him no walls for solitude – just a network of shared desks and people – mostly – minding their own business. Only team leads got their own offices.

So, focus he must.

He drew in deep, slow breaths, eyes closed. Perhaps to others it would seem he was overwhelmed by the gore.

Then again, this was a particularly difficult group of people to keep behavioral secrets from.

So, he needed. To. *Focus*.

When his breath fell under control again, he hit play, pencil still poised for note-taking.

And Show started to dance again.

Long, slow cuts. Carving off long strips or leaving simple slices.

With each few strokes, they would wander behind the captive, knife brushing across the linen canvasing the background, letting the blood soak in in simple, dark streaks.

One by one by one by one by one, the strikes of blood littered the canvas. At first, they seemed to be building toward a design. A message. A purpose.

But more built – as they always did – building and building and building upon each other. Overlapping and crossing and dripping down.

Only once the entire canvas was evenly coated in red did Showoff finally let the sobbing man die, pulling out the gag and dragging his head up to center by a firm, gloved grip on his hair.

Forcing his eyes to the camera.

The man tried to sputter a plea – something.

The words were lost to pain, blood loss, and terror.

The knife slashed across his throat.

Eyes grew wild and wide with panic as he resumed his groggy thrashing, desperate gurgles spewing from his throat as blood poured and spurted away, retreating down his bare chest littered in cuts and stripes of exposed muscle.

Darian's heart was pounding so loud in his chest he could swear the rest of the team could hear it, eyes glued to the screen as shame and dread crawled up his stomach. Not the dread of this scene. Not empathy or horror. The dread of being caught. Of someone having some impossible mind reading ability – someone knowing how sick he was for being so addicted to this.

He just kept watching – he couldn't bring himself to pause it even as his breaths grew tighter and faster.

As the man choked out, Show didn't do anything. They just kept their blank-masked face tipped up toward the camera as their hand drifted slowly through the man's hair again and again, following smoothly and simply however he thrashed trying to avoid it.

Eventually, delirious and fading fast, he leaned into it.

They always did.

Show didn't stop his head from dropping to his chest when what remained of his strength faded away.

Their head turned to regard the not-quite-dead-yet man momentarily, then their face pulled back up to stare directly into the camera again.

Darian's stomach was flipping. As if Show could see straight through time. Through the frame. Through the glass. Into the darkest, coldest corner of his soul.

Show did as they always did.

They stepped forward, bending until the mask all but filled the frame.

Then, slowly – a single leather-clad thumb lifted into view. It smeared across the frame, leaving it streaked with dark, sloppy red.

The video ended. Clipped to the first frame and a play button.

Darian pulled in a deep, painful breath, struggling to keep his expression neutral.

His hands moved on their own, blindly as his eyes stayed on the screen. They slid open a drawer of his desk and plucked up a new flash drive.

Then plugged it into his laptop next to the other.

Systematically, he duplicated the video file onto the fresh flash drive, then ejected it.

Paranoia prickled at Darian's mind as his eyes made a quick survey of the office – making sure no one was watching as he slipped the pirated video into his pocket to bring home.

He'd watch it again and write up the report. Do his job. Shut down his thoughts.

But Darian needed to see that again. Alone.

2

— · —

PRIVATE SHOWING

The families.

Darian pondered what they were doing now. He wondered if, maybe, they made copies of the videos themselves before they turned the tape in to the police.

He wondered how long they stared in abject horror at the screen before calling the police.

If they watched it all the way through. If they got so far as to see Show prowling up to the camera, masked face tilting ever so slightly – as if they saw straight through the family's screen and into them.

If they flinched when Show smeared blood over the lens.

He wondered, vaguely, if any of them were a little twisted like him. If not twisted, then ... obsessive, maybe. Desperate enough to find the killer that they wanted to analyze it. Or, maybe, just so distraught that their husband, boyfriend, son, cousin, co-worker, whatever the victim was to them, spent his last forty-two minutes and seventeen seconds in horror-stricken, agonized loneliness, that they made copies too. Watched it back over and over and over again.

Staring at the screen with a beer and bleary eyes that had long given up screaming for sleep and settled into silent, watering acquiescence.

Staring at the victim.

Just him and the knife.

The knife and the elegance of the silent knife wielder.

Darian couldn't get the image of the families out of his head. He'd put in a request a few times now to be the first on the scene, but local officers always picked up the case to confirm that it really was Showoff and not some other killer or a sick prank. Only *then* would they pass it off to the BAU and it would land on Darian's desk.

It was a crock of shit.

He needed to be able to see the families. He wanted to be able to see their reactions. Were they crying as they handed over the tape? Were their eyes glazed and hollow as they robotically invited the officers in and systematically poured coffee for their guests, desperately clinging to the gilded decorum rather than drown in the vast unknown grief?

Maybe they were glad. Possibly. Plenty of families have squabbles, affairs, inheritance fights, or who knows what else preceding this. Maybe their poor victim wasn't so loved after all.

Darian was still pissed he didn't get to see. He got to talk to them later, sure, but there wasn't really a way for him to know what they were like in *that* moment. He wanted to know if they wailed in their grief.

For this. For his work.

Of course.

It was important for the case. Important for the profile. Any other reasonings or obsessions he might have surrounding the situation were purely coincidental and not in any way a driving reason for his repeated requests.

Mmm ...

His internal wrestle with phrasings stumbled to a stop as Show's knife blotted the final stain of red into place, soaking through the last of the draped linen.

They were beautiful on the screen.

Well. Not a *screen*. Not this time.

Darian didn't dare watch these little home videos upstairs in sight of the windows whose shutters he never quite trusted. He'd much rather analyze them in the basement from the comfort of his secondhand couch. A small projector haphazardly screwed into the exposed beams of the unfinished basement, a white sheet draping over a blank section of wall became his screen, and a minifridge next to the couch served both as end table and beer cooler.

Forty-two minutes and seventeen seconds.

They were thirty-eight minutes and forty-eight seconds in now as Darian cracked open another bottle, flicking the cap across the cement floor – eyes never leaving the screen.

11

He wondered just how freaked out the victim – this one's name was 'Marcus', by the way – would be if he knew what the video was for. If it had been explained to him. If Show was gracious enough to tell Marc that the video would be sent to his family. Then the police station. Then the FBI.

He wondered if poor Marc ever quite grasped the concept of how many people would be watching this. Or – on top of that – how many people like Darian (or the potential, aforementioned family members) would make copies to watch over. And over. And over.

Maybe someday, Showoff's work would even get one of those serial killer documentaries. Darian assumed it would – they were already up to eighteen documented kills. Plus, movie-makers have a flare for showcasing people who have a flare for the cinematic.

Poor Marcus' screams might be on Netflix someday, labeled with a simple '*This episode contains graphic depictions of a murder – viewer discretion advised.*'

As if anyone ever 'discresses' with that.

They all watch it – just like Darian did. So many people are obsessed with serial killer documentaries and true crime podcasts – Darian wasn't so different. Preferring one object of fascination and preferring the uncut content was just a quirk of his.

This was normal.

Normal how he leaned forward, adrenaline pumping through his veins as Show brought the knife to Marcus' throat. Again. For the twelfth time this night since Darian set the application to play on loop hours ago.

Darian stood, stepping closer to watch as the knife melted through flesh, blood spurting through gargles and wordless pleas. The rush was fading by quite a bit this time – he knew this scene too well now – but that didn't mean it wasn't *good*. It still made him dizzy with a soft, empowered pleasure as Marc sputtered out, crimson soaking down his slaughtered chest.

Darian's eyes were on Show now, though, as his target approached the camera.

He squinted, trying so *so* hard to see Show's eyes through the holes in the mask.

The inside must have been lined with black mesh.

As Show stared back at him, a murmur pressed unbidden from Darian's lips.

"I will find you."

There was the smallest beat of silence – as if Show were sizing him up. Analyzing the words and the man behind them.

Then. As always. Their thumb smudged red across the screen, blinking them into darkness yet again.

3

CUE CARD

The letter didn't have a return address. Didn't have postage. Didn't have much bulk to it at all.

Confused, Darian slid it from his mailbox, peeking inside to ensure he didn't miss another bill – or, heaven forbid, another fucking round of advertisements – before stopping to flip the envelope over.

It was blank.

Tied up in rusty red string.

No ... is that ... was that ... fabric? Strips of fabr –

His hands, body, and mind locked in place all at once.

Linen.

Linen – he was right – it was linen. The blood-soaked linen from Showoff's videos –

Fuck.

Darian took a desperate glance up the street, then jogged to the end of his sidewalk, head tossing back and forth. He frantically searched the road and memorized the cars. Looking for anyone suspicious. Anyone with a hood up or ... or who didn't seem to belong there.

Nothing.

Fucking *nothing* – how long had this been there?

FUCK.

His breath and hands were both moving again now – both shaky as he turned the envelope over in his hand.

He ran back inside, slamming the door behind him. The letter slid onto the table as he quickly found gloves and awkwardly fumbled them on with frantically flexing fingers. He re-approached, sliding a butter knife under the paper to pry away the glue with as little damage as possible.

Should he be bringing this into the office? Yes. Could it be stuffed with anthrax or who fucking knows what? Also yes.

But. Darian could just tell them he didn't realize the letter was from Show until it was opened – that he didn't recognize the fabric when it was cut so thin.

He could do that.

That was reasonable – people who didn't spend all-nighters staring at the videos wouldn't have noticed.

He ...

... he had spent *all night* watching the video.

He'd spent all night watching the *fucking* video and this was *right fuckin' there* in the morning.

Show had been there. Show had been there while *he* was *there*. While he was there watching the *fucking* video – *fuck* –

15

... Darian would need to triple-check the blackoutability of the basement curtains after this.

He was so fucking screwed if Show saw him –

ANYWAY –

Shaking fingers pulled out the small paper, turning it over.

Aaaaand this dude was a classic.

Cutout letters from magazines. Of course.

Darian's eyes skimmed the single sentence.

a FOx RArELy ExpEcts its HouND

TO bE as PREtTY As yOU <3

Darian ... froze.

Staring.

Breath locked up and stuck in his lungs.

Whatever he had expected, that wasn't it.

Fuck.

4

— · —

MANDATORY UNAUTHORIZED RESEARCH MONTAGE

'*Off the case.*' What the hell did they mean, '*off the case*'? Darian didn't understand for a long few seconds, sputtering excuses in the director's office. *He* was the lead on this unsub. *He* had the most information. *He* had been tracking them for *years*. Now, all of a sudden, just because Showoff had sent him a letter, he wasn't allowed to track the fucker down anymore?

That didn't even make *sense*. The director said it was a "safety concern." That having the unsub obsessed with him was a "danger."

But if Show was a danger, wouldn't they have come *into* the house? Wouldn't they have knocked on his door or crept in through the window? Strangled or shot him in his sleep?

They didn't. All they did was leave a note saying he was cute and move on. Darian didn't see how that was enough of a concern to take him off the *case*. It seemed pointless, cowardly, and generally stupid. Wasn't his job dangerous *every* day? Didn't this make him the best lead they'd had?

Darian regretted even telling them as he shoved clothes into his suitcase back home. He couldn't even stay in his own damn *house* now.

He shouldn't have told them. Shouldn't have brought the letter there in the first place. It was a snap decision. Made before he could even get a word in about it. The director simply made her swift and ruthless judgment, gavel crashing down on years of obsession and aspirations.

"I ... I don't know that it was them – ! It could be a prank! Just some stupid kids–"

"–Oh, please, Shah. Don't be reckless – if a killer is targeting you, you need to take a step back. If they're trying to impress you or lure you in, you could set them into a spree. You know *that."*

Darian's hand had curled around the plastic-bound linen strips in his pocket. He was going to give them to her, but at this point, the less evidence he had to support that it was really a *killer* sending him the letter, the more likely he'd be able to talk his way back onto the team.

They wouldn't know what to do with the strips of linen, anyway. They'd just confirm that it was one of the victims' blood and keep it in evidence for when they eventually caught this bastard. What else could you possibly learn fr –

Darian stopped in the middle of shoving toiletries into the front pocket of the suitcase, staring blankly at the floor.

There *was* something you could learn from it ...

Darian skipped downstairs – he'd have to destroy all evidence of him keeping Show's movies, anyway. Glad he hadn't done that yet, Darian shoved a flash drive into his projector and slapped the lights off. A random film of Showoff's started playing – one from six months ago. The victim – Carmen, this one's name was – struggled in her chair as she always did, but this time, Darian's eyes were locked onto the linen sheet.

It was a rough estimate, but he traced the outlines of the cloth. It was tall as well as wide, covering the entire frame and then some. No seams. No connections. It was over two yards tall. It *had* to be.

A grin curled over Darian's lips. Because how many places carried linen you could buy with more than two yards of height in this city?

The rest of the afternoon was a frenzied blur. Darian shoved the souvenirs and snuff films into his bag to take them with him, finished packing quickly, and threw everything roughly into the backseat of his truck. Within an hour, he'd been at three craft stores already, combing through to find bolts of linen.

Bolt after bolt was wrong. Too white. Too brown. Too low a thread count. Too high a threat count. Too short a cut.

By the seventh craft store, it was already eight P.M. and employees were getting tired and less willing to assist him.

But he found it.

In the back corner of a little family-owned shop on the old main street, Darian finally found just the right bolt of linen. He pressed the small plastic evidence bag against the fabric, lining up the threaded, bloody grid of the sample piece with the fresh, bright linen on the bolt.

It was a perfect match. The sample he had was slightly misshapen from blood and stretching, but the threads lined up almost perfectly regardless, and the color of the bolt matched the hue he remembered from the films.

Darian was locked in place as the ramifications bled through his mind. If he could track the right sales to the right buyer, that would be it. Show would be caught. Put in prison.

The snuff films would be done.

...Why did that leave such a hollow pit in his stomach? Wasn't it a *good* thing that this motherfucker was going to be behind bars? That no family would ever be forced to watch a video of their child, spouse, parent, or friend being mutilated for a silent, shadowed, and faceless killer?

It crossed his mind a few times that he *could* just put the bolt back. Go to his hotel like he was supposed to. Let the nitwits who were taking over *his* case fail again and again and again.

But he couldn't bring himself to be out of the loop. Couldn't imagine not seeing the videos or knowing their progress. Besides, more people were going to die if he didn't do anything about this, and it was his job to save them.

Mind set, he tucked the bolt of linen under his arm and moved up through the cramped hobby shop and set it on the front counter.

The girl behind it perked up, popping her earbuds out with a startled smile. "Oh – ! Hi! I can get this cut for you – how many yards do you need?" She moved her phone under the counter and stood to pull the bolt to her chest.

Darian put a hand on it, stopping her. "I don't need any. I'd like to get some sales information from you." He flipped open his badge for her to see. "FBI. I need to know who has bought this fabric in the past two years."

The girl blinked at him in a confused flutter. "Oh – Oh, um – ... ssssure?" She side-stepped to the computer and opened up the program, dipping a few times to read the numbers on the label. "What's this for?" she queried, voice half-distracted as she scrolled through options and grids on her screen.

"That's classified, I'm sorry."

"Okayyyy – anything specific I'm looking for? There's quite a few on here – "

Darian hummed, thinking. "It'd be more than four yards at each sale, possibly doubled on some purchases, but no more than that. You can cut out credit card sales – we're looking for cash only." He severely doubted Show was stupid enough to pay for murder materials with a card.

"Okay ... ummmm – yeah, there – I flagged all the cash sales over forty dollars for you. Want me to print this out?"

"That works fine, thanks." Darian eyed the red-dotted camera that was pointed at his face from behind the cashier. "Let me see the security footage as well."

She frowned, glancing behind her. "I'm so sorry – this one's fake, actually, but there's stuff in the parking lot?"

Darian found himself frowning. He didn't have *time* to go through city protocol. "How about the people next door?"

"Umm – " She looked up as the printer under the counter started whirring and clicking. Glancing toward the door. "I thiiiiiink so? It's some bigger chains, so they can probably afford it?"

"Perfect, thank you – " Darian took the paper as she offered it to him, glancing over the sales. There couldn't be more than two hundred here. Good. "Jot down your name and number for me, too. I might have more questions."

"Oh – ! Sure, yeah – one sec – " She scribbled down the note on a fresh piece of printer paper and handed that to him, too. "Any way I can help, just lemme know!"

"I appreciate that. Have a good evening, miss." He took the paper and headed out the door.

It only took a few quick glances to see who in the area had cameras pointed toward the parking lot. He'd check there in a moment.

His eyes skimmed the page quickly, marking off all sales within a week of any of the kills.

Within the first four, he'd found the pattern. Someone bought a four-yard by two-yard piece in the late morning the day before each kill. Every. Single. Time.

Darian's heart was beating a bit quicker as he thumbed through the pages, circling date after date after date. The times. All paid in cash. All the same amount. *Always* the day before the kills.

Incredible. Darian was grinning like a schoolboy over the pages as the pattern unraveled in front of him. The grin snapped away again as he noticed the last entry on the sales list.

The same timeframe.

Same size.

Bought yesterday.

5

SECURITY

Darian always had a knack for spelling. Ever since he was a young child, it never quite made sense to him why someone should 'sound out' a word. His classmates would be writing out 'chruck' and 'chree' or 'twuck' and 'twee' from using their ears. Darian, somehow, just remembered where the letters went. Which letters were friends and which made what sounds together. 'Sounding' something out too often led to incorrect results. So, he'd simply copy the word down over and over and over again until it stuck in his brain.

As a seven-year-old, Darian almost never colored or drew with the other kids. Instead, he'd spend his time writing down all the words he saw around him in no particular order. Notebooks and notebooks piled up in his closet, written in crayon, pen, marker, and colored pencil with thousands of random words he'd come across in his time.

He was the best speller in school, so when the idea of a 'spelling bee' was brought to his attention in fourth grade, little Darian had jumped at the opportunity, signing up immediately.

It sounded like a fine idea. Someone asks you how to spell something, and you do it. He looked through a list of common spelling bee words and wrote them again and again to remember them. He wrote them at the dinner table. He finger-spelled them in his poor, clunky sign language when he wasn't allowed to write in church. He wrote them in the margins of his homework and in the dirt of the playground fence line.

Yet, somehow, the actual competition was so much more difficult than he imagined.

In short, Darian did not win. In long, Darian took one look at the crowd gathered below the stage and vomited onto the only microphone the school could afford, ruining the night for everyone and earning himself even more horrid nicknames at school.

Darian never tried to go on stage again after that. Never tried public speaking. Never signed up for school plays or choirs. When he was forced to participate, Darian would request to be 'Tree #4' or whatever part had little to no speaking lines and would squeeze his eyes shut whenever he absolutely *had* to speak on stage.

Darian couldn't imagine how Show did it. It made plenty of sense to want to be seen and known and understood, yet the thought of being filmed while doing something so intimate seemed atrocious to Darian. He would sooner film for a porno than a murder. In porn, you show more body than soul.

Darian wasn't sure what he'd do if that much of his soul were on display for the world to see, scrutinized and studied by agents like himself. At least on stage, it was one showing, then you were done. On film, anyone could watch it again and again and again. Any mistakes would be recorded forever, infinite and immortal. That was something Darian could never understand. What if there were mistakes? What if everyone judged you?

All this musing was to say that Darian was *deeply* uncomfortable each time he checked security cameras. Seeing himself on the footage when he'd barely even registered that the cameras existed in the first place was nauseating.

He'd successfully talked his way into the shop's office and gotten access to their security footage. After the clerk gave him a quick rundown of how to use the application and search for dates and times, they had run away again to help customers, leaving Darian blessedly alone.

Of course, the most recent event caught on camera was Darian walking into the shop and talking to the clerk, so that was the first thing that showed up on the screen. Darian couldn't keep himself from hitting play to watch the interaction, grimacing at the way he moved and spoke and the little nervous twitch that kept his knuckles coming back up to his jaw, rubbing at it pointlessly.

It was painful to watch. It made him sick.

He thought of Show in comparison. How seamless and elegant their every move was. They were smoke tumbling through a gentle breeze, and he was a clatter of pots and pans banging down a rusted and rotting staircase.

Somehow, it made him feel far more like 'Barf-face' than 'Agent Shah.' If he was going to take down Show, he *needed* to be Agent Shah. Still, he was left with a pit of self-loathing and anxiety.

Swallowing thickly, he forced himself through the work. He flipped through the folders of recordings until he located the camera pointed toward the parking lot. Then, he scrolled to the date and time of the first sale.

He stopped breathing as the customer moved across the grainy screen, shopping bag in hand.

They were smaller than he'd imagined them. Curling hair fell just to their shoulders in a cool, faded auburn.

He played it again.

Again and again and again.

Even without seeing their face; even without checking the other times; even without waiting for another body to come on screen, Darian knew that was Show.

No one else on this planet could glide over solid ground that gracefully.

Darian blew up the image and jotted down the license plate number of the hatchback Show climbed into. He barely remembered to scoop up his papers before he was out the door and bolting for the car.

Maybe a better man would have stopped to think about reporting it to his supervisor.

Darian just looked up the address in a blur, then made a beeline to the highway with a pounding heart and loaded gun.

6

‑ ∶ ‑

SHOWING LIVE

Darian just –

Stared.

He should have said something.

He should have said '*FBI – PUT DOWN THE WEAPON!*'

It wasn't like he hadn't done that before.

Still, the words died on his tongue, sliding back down his throat and rotting in his twisting stomach as he stared at the scene before him.

A chair. A camera.

A man in the chair. Bleeding heavily, of course.

And Showoff.

Show and their glistening blade, paused mid-cut as their eyes undoubtedly found Darian through the black mesh in their mask.

The victim stared at Darian too, pleas and crackling screams muffled and lost into the fabric of the gag.

But the door was behind the camera. Perfectly so.

To anyone watching, it would seem the victim was just ... pleading at his audience. Begging for it to be a livestream. For someone to rescue him.

No words came out formed enough to communicate in the slightest.

... No one knew.

No one would know.

No one had to know he was there.

He should say the words.

He didn't.

Darian should shoot.

The gun lowered through the air instead until it came to rest pointed limply at the ground.

His eyes never left Show.

Show stayed still for a long few moments, masked face still pointed toward the intruding officer.

Then. Slowly. They continued to carve.

A tangle of emotions rang through Darian's blood.

He had to kill Show now. He had to. If he didn't, Show would tell everyone how he didn't stop them. They would know how Darian stared. They would know what he was.

... His fingers rippled over the handle of the gun.

Show's movements slowed slightly ... then the knife twisted.

A cry cracked up the man's throat, sending him into a sputtering, agonized wail that tapered into choked coughs.

... The gun lowered again.

And Show moved on. Finally turning their back to Darian – decided he wasn't a threat in that moment and just ... *moved on*.

Darian's heart slammed in his chest, searching the eyes of the man. Darian didn't even know his name. This poor, innocent (probably? Darian had no way to know for sure) man was going to die.

He was going to die as an FBI agent watched.

Doing nothing.

Doing nothing but trying to keep his expression neutral.

Doing nothing but trying *not* to watch.

Trying not to inhale ecstasy at every scream.

They were so much *better* here.

The screams didn't just have pitch and volume. They had body. They had *life* and *desperation* and *form*. They danced around the room, a surround sound symphony of iniquity and desperation.

Darian tried.

He *tried*.

Oh, how he tried.

He tried to lift the gun. To point it at Show. To find a way to get out of here. To play the hero even when he came without telling his team he'd found a lead. Came here knowing he wanted to see Show alone.

Came ... wanting to see this.

No.

No, he'd wanted to *stop* this. Of *course* he'd wanted to stop this – the only reason he hadn't told anyone on his team was because they'd have simply taken too long to get there, anyway, and he was better off using what precious little time he had getting to the scene and saving this poor man's life.

That's why he came alone.

That's why he broke protocol.

For the invaluable life of the man in the ch –

... Darian flinched as the knife ripped across the man's throat.

***

Everything was a bit of a blur after that.

Numbness set in. Something twixt self-loathing and disbelief that he'd actually let that happen. Then he realized just how *much* he'd watched. How long he'd mindlessly stared as the room smelled more and more like blood. As the barely streaked linen draped behind the pair slowly soaked through with crimson until its steady drips were the only sound in the room.

The camera turned off.

The man stopped breathing. Stopped twitching. Stopped living.

Because of him.

Because he didn't stop it.

And now the two were alone.

Darian's mind clawed back up from the fog as Show stepped around the camera, looking him over. Their face was still covered, but Darian could feel their eyes dragging up every inch of his body as they stepped closer. Slow and deliberate. Light on their feet as always.

Even more graceful in person. The camera didn't do them justice.

Darian found himself taking a shaky, half-step back. His gun raised again. Form? Bad. But the end that goes 'BANG' was pointed at Show. Good enough.

Show froze at the sight of the gun, face tilting down to the knife that still clung to their hand. Carefully, they reached far to the side, setting it down on the ground.

Then nudging it away with their foot.

Darian drew in a long breath, trying to keep it even. " ... *The mask.*"

Show's head tilted almost playfully to the side. Carefully – likely just moving slowly so they didn't spook Darian into pulling the trigger – they gestured to the gun.

" ... *What?*" His voice was just a whisper – why couldn't he get it to *work* – ?

They just gestured again.

... Mmmask off if he puts the gun down?

Darian frowned, fingers flexing around the glock. " ... Step back a little."

Show shrugged, hands out at their sides in a soft surrender. They slid back a couple feet, then crossed their arms. Waiting.

… This was so stupid. So fucking stupid – he couldn't just …

He should be shooting Show right now. He should be putting a bullet through their head he could say he came in at the last minute and they tried to run he could *still* fix this he … he could … he …

He lowered the gun. Slowly.

Safety on, then set it on the ground.

Show stared.

… Darian slid it to the other side of the room with his foot.

The smile practically bled through the damn mask as Show nodded in approval. Their hands came together, first peeling back the leather driving gloves they were so fond of. Or … maybe not so fond – they just tossed them across the room in little bloody wads.

Then, slender fingers picked at the black spandex material under their mask – pulling it away from the neck, then up over their face.

Darian didn't know what he'd expected Show to look like.

This wasn't it. Yet … seeing them shake out their curls and give him a bright, lopsided grin, Darian didn't know how he could ever picture them looking any other way.

Their eyes were bright. Face young. Hair a mess of curls that dropped to their shoulders in a color so similar to his grandmother's molasses cookies, he could practically see the grains of sugar on Show's cheeks dappled in amongst the scars that slashed through clear skin.

Show didn't stop, unzipping their hoodie and shrugging it off. Then the next one that hid beneath. They must have been fucking dying in all those layers – *damn*.

"Not gonna say anything?"

Darian almost flinched when Show spoke. It was so clear. So casual. So unfettered by the hour of unuse.

Darian suddenly ... didn't know what to do with his hands. No gun? No gun. Pppppppockets? No.

Folded. Arms folded.

That'd work.

Show rolled their eyes, tossing the bundle of clothes onto the couch – this basement functioned more like a studio apartment than anything – then wandered toward the fridge in the kitchenette. "I know you drink Corona, but I have Blue Moon. Tragedy for you."

Darian almost dropped the fucking bottle that hurtled through the air at him moments later.

He didn't – the glass caught in his useless fucking hands – almost slipping, but not.

Cold.

Show just laughed at him, cracking the top of their own open against the countertop. "Wow – you're really shaken, huh? Not like you haven't seen any of that before."

Darian ... was ...

What the fuck was he supposed to be doing here?

Were they having a *conversation* now?

What the fuck was going on?

He stared down at the beer in his hands. And said the ... well, the only thing that came to mind.

" ... Are you a hipster or something?"

Amusement and wonder flickered across Show's eyes. " ... Because of the beer?"

"Yeah."

They shrugged, hopping up onto the counter and tipping the bottle up in a sip. "Not sure. Depends on your definition of 'hipster.' I hate flannel though, and beanies hate me, so that's not a good start." They glanced down to the bottle in Darian's hands. " ... Yyyyyyyou want me to open that for you?"

Darian didn't even want to drink something Show gave him. That would be incredibly stupid – it could be drugged or something.

The fucking mind reader piped up. "It's literally factory sealed, it's *fine*."

Darian eyed Show, but found his hand moving toward his pocket. He slipped out his keys, cracked open the top, and gestured to it. "Happy?"

Show grinned at him, taking a sip of their own beer. "*Very*, thank you~"

Darian didn't drink. Not that brave yet.

Which was fucking stupid. Show was right, it was sealed. It was new. It was *fine*. It's fine. It's *fine, stopfreakingout* –

He watched Show for a few moments longer as the bottle rolled back and forth in his hands. " ... What's your name?"

Show sputtered a laugh, almost losing beer there. They wiped their mouth on the back of their hand as their legs swung back and forth. "*Seriously*? You tracked me the fuck down and you don't even know my name? How is that even possible?"

Darian glared to the side – at the wall. Toward the ground. " ... Didn't run the paper check, I just followed."

Show smirked. "Riiiiiight~ You were keeping this excursion from your supervisors. *Very* sexy. I approve."

Darian's glare flicked back up to Show. "Are you going to tell me or not?"

Show shrugged. "Not like you can't get it in like ... ten seconds by Googling what you already know. *Buttttttttttttttt*. Fine, sure. My name's Calyx."

Darian rolled the syllables around in his mouth. Trying them. Tasting them. " ... Calyx ... is that your legal name?"

Show nodded. "Had it for years, yeah."

Darian's lips pinched together, looking at his beer. " ... You weren't even on my list."

Sho – no, *Calyx* – grinned at him. "Yeah? *Fantastic*. Do I get a sticker?" Another swig.

Darian's eyes slid to the body on the other side of the room. Blood was still oozing from it, sliding in long, sticky drips to the puddle on the ground. " ... Why are you doing this?"

Show – no, *CALYX*. Calyx. Calyx raised a brow at him. "Why do I kill ... ? What are you, a shrink?"

" ... No, I meant – why ... " Geez, now he just felt stupid. " ... Why ... are we ... talking ... ?" Gesturing awkwardly to the beer.

Calyx burst into laughter, curling up around their bottle. "*Woooooooooowwwwwww* – wow, you don't even *care*, do you? You're *really* fucked up, dude~!"

Darian's cheeks burned, shame clawing up his throat. "Th – ... no? No, that's not even what I'm talking ab – "

"*Shhhtshstshtshtshtttt~*" Calyx waved a fluttering hand in his direction. "I'm fucked up too, you're fine. That's your answer. I'm not gonna kill my favorite viewer. We can hang out for a while and sate each other's curiosity and tomorrow we can go back to the little cat and mouse game and it'll be *fine~*" The bottle lifted to their lips again. "You worry too much, dude."

Darian frowned at them, but found the beer on his tongue as well.

... It was good. It soothed him. An old friend – maybe with a different twist, but still much the same. Comforting.

... He glanced toward the door.

Then to the clock.

" ... Truce for tonight?"

Calyx smirked up at him. "Deal. A *real* truce, though. No using things you learned here against me and I won't do the same to you. Mutually assured destruction."

Darian drew in a long breath, nodding. He downed another few icy pulls on the bottle, bracing himself for this insanity.

" ... Okay. Um ... wh – "

"No no no – you already got a question in. My turn."

Darian rolled his eyes, moving to perch on the edge of the table now. A little closer. "Fine. What's your question?"

"Are you single?"

Darian almost choked. "I – why does that matter?"

Calyx shrugged. "Matters cuz I wanna know."

He sighed. "I'm married to my work."

"*Awwwhhhh~* You're basically married to *me* then, huh, hubby?"

Darian must have made some kind of amusing expression in response to that, because Calyx was *immediately* victim to a burst of laughter again. "No, really, though – ! You're obsessed with me – I know you are. Just admit itttttt~"

Darian's eyes narrowed slightly. He decided to just move on from that. "How many have you killed?"

Calyx's head tilted back and forth in thought. "Tricky question."

"How the everloving fuck is that a tricky question?"

Calyx gasped in offense. "Because you didn't clarify intent or ... or causation? I have *categories.*"

Darian rolled his eyes. "Okay, how about two numbers – one for total people who would probably be alive if it weren't for you, and one for full-on first-degree premeditated shit?" That sentence slid from his lips so smoothly, Darian was almost worried.

… He was already far too casual around Calyx.

He forced himself to look at the mutilated corpse in the room.

See that, Darian? *That's* what happens when you get stupid around an unsub.

Be smarter.

Calyx cut off his thoughts with numbers. "M'kay, uhhh … total issssss … twenty-five. First-degree, twenty-one."

Darian frowned, eyes turning back to them. "I only have nineteen videos, counting this one."

Calyx shrugged. "Didn't get my vibe going for a minute. First couple were sloppy."

… Darian didn't know what to say to that, so he just … found himself drinking again. Stomach twisting.

Calyx hummed, feet kicking in a smooth rhythm as they pondered the next question. "Mmm … how 'boutttttt … hmm … know what? Same question. What's your body count?"

Darian sighed. Thinking.

Ignoring the double meaning. This game sucked.

" … Killed three. One on accident, two on the job."

"OoooOOoooo~ *Very* scary. Very cool. You look sexy in the bulletproof vest, by the way." Calyx gestured toward Darian's chest with their beer.

... Suddenly Darian wanted it off. Or ... on more? More on him but not – Actually, maybe just something else on him? Something more. Something not that. " ... Thanks."

Deeeeeep breath. Another drink.

Focus. Think.

"What do you do for a living?"

Calyx lit up a little. "Aww~! Cute question! I'm a dancer."

An error screen practically scrolled across Darian's eyes. " ... Dance ... *fuck*, that should have been obvious ... " Why hadn't he *thought* of that?

Calyx laughed, looking over him. "Why?"

Darian gestured vaguely toward Calyx. A little sloppy in the gestures – apparently not putting in much effort. "Cuz you're ... like ... I dunno, smooth? Graceful and ... shit ... ?"

Calyx pressed a hand to their heart. "*Awwwwhhhh,* really~?"

Darian nodded, setting the beer to the side.

That stuff was shit, it was giving him a headache. And ... kinda a stomachache?

Ew. Moving on. "Next question?"

Calyx chewed on their lip as they thought, sliding off the counter in favor of leaning against it. "Hmm*mmm* ... oh – ! Which of my videos is your favorite?"

Whyyyyy was Darian still here?

41

He could leave.

He *should* leave. He should leave.

Why wasn't he leaving – ? What the fuck was wrong with him.

Darian glowered at them. "I don't have a favorite. It's not something I enjoy."

Calyx rolled their eyes, stepping closer. "We both know that's a lie, Agent~" Darian flinched backward as Calyx booped his nose.

Darian refused to back away. Calyx ... was incredibly close – wayyyyyy too fucking close, their legs were almost touching –

But he wasn't going to be a little bitch and shrink away from someone so much smaller than him. It was *fine.* He was fine. This was fine.

" ... Rachel Wheeler."

A smirk crackled across Calyx's lips. "The garotte?"

Darian gave a small shrug, finding his hand around the bottle again. He needed something to hold. Something to focus the nervous energy on. " ... Good sounds," he muttered, taking another swig.

Calyx was grinning again. "They really were, weren't they? I should work that angle more often."

Darian rolled his eyes. "You're not going to be doing this much longer."

Calyx's brows popped up. "Why? Cuz *you're* going to stop me?"

Darian tried to glare past the sarcasm. "That's about right, yeah."

"*I've been really loving watching you try~*" Smirking now. Stepping closer until their leg brushed the inside of Darian's thigh. Smirk growing as Darian squirmed a little, eyes flitting away.

" ... Do you ... have – l-ike *no* idea what personal space is – ?" Leaning back a little. Heart slamming sirens into his mind.

Calyx hummed in thought, hand smoothing over Darian's chest to hook two fingers into the top of his vest. "Mmmm*nope~* Never heard of it." They reeled him back the few inches he'd retreated.

Darian's eyes turned up to Calyx's again, searching their face. " ... I agreed to conversation, n-ot touching."

Calyx chuckled softly, thumb brushing over the bit of collarbone that showed around his shirt collar. "Oh, come *on~* Not like I could hurt you. You're like twice my size with combat training." They took a moment to tug the collar of Darian's shirt straight, smoothing down the fabric. "You could stop me *any* time."

Darian just ... stared.

Calyx leaned in, looking very pleased with themself as they nuzzled their nose behind Darian's ear.

Panic and excitement and worry and fascination clashed inside of him, slamming his heart against his ribs and curling his fingers tighter around the almost-empty bottle.

He felt hot.

Too hot.

Almost light-headed as his head tilted just a little away. " ... *I don't want to hurt you.*"

A grin spread against his scalp. "*I like your shampoo.*"

... He was being sniffed.

........greattttttttttt –

" ... *Thanks.*" He forced the bottle up and took another drink, immediately grimacing at how it churned inside his stomach.

He set down the b –

... The sound of shattering glass echoed in the room, slamming against the inside of his skull.

Calyx pulled back, glancing down to the bottle that had slipped from Darian's fingers. "Well, that's a mess."

Darian stared too.

How did he ... he wouldn't have dropped that. He ...

He rubbed his fingers together, breath immediately locking up in his throat as he realized.

They were numb.

Alarm bells that were distant in the back of his mind were starting to come to the front now as he twisted, staring behind him to see the length of the room.

... Vision swimming – fuck.

Fuck fuck fuck *fuck FUCK* –

He stared at the bottle for another moment.

Not factory sealed. *Re*sealed.

FUCK.

Darian immediately tried to stand straight, toppling backward *far* too easily as Calyx's hand shoved at his chest, pinning him there.

"Awwww – I'm sorry, is that *scary*? Honestly I'm surprised you actually drank that, it was just a shot in the dark." Darian flinched as Calyx's hand ghosted over his cheek, cradling it and wiping over the skin with a thumb.

The world was already spinning so bad – his hand tried to shove at Calyx, but mostly ended up focused on gripping the edge of the table, eyes blinking hard through the sludge and the fog that was quickly flooding through his mind. "*Ffffuckking bitch –* "

Calyx's laughter filled his ears again. Lips pressed to his cheek. "Don't be like that, baby. You liked my movies so much, I just figured you'd like to be in one~"

7

STARDOM

Darian woke slowly – then all at once, grimacing as a foul odor shoved into his sinuses and twisted his stomach, zapping panic, consciousness, and unease through his mind. He turned his head, neck aching from drooping, and coughed away the scent.

"*Theeeeere* you are~"

Darian twitched as a hand patted his cheek.

He took a few heaving breaths before turning his eyes up to Calyx – the little shit was straddling him.

... He was in a chair. Wooden chair. Wrists tied behind the back.

The corners of the wood bruised into his arms and shoulder blades – far too tight. His back arched to alleviate a bit of the stretch as his hands fisted and squirmed, trying to wriggle away from the ropes or at *least* find a knot he could reach enough to pick at.

He found nothing.

He got nowhere.

Calyx's hands smoothed up his chest – it was bare now – both the Kevlar vest and his fucking *shirt* were gone.

Creep.

"You sure are pretty," Calyx murmured, palming up Darian's throat.

Darian's head wrenched away from the touch. "G-et *off* me – "

Calyx just breathed a twinkling laugh, hands running through Darian's hair now instead. "Nahhhhhhhhhhh – I'm savoring this."

Darian's eyes slid away from Calyx's, trying to press away the last of the fog from his mind. Looking at *literally* anyth –

... His stomach twisted as he caught a glimpse of the camera over Calyx's shoulder. Not on. Not blinking red.

But pointed right at him.

Breath caught painfully in his lungs as he twisted his head back, staring behind them for th –

... Y-yeah. Yeah, that was ... that was a new drape of linen.

Clean.

White.

Ready for blood.

His blood.

Darian couldn't quite keep the panic out of his eyes as he looked back over Calyx. They were in the 'Showoff' outfit again. Layered in black, loose fabric. Everything but the mask and gloves.

47

Calyx smirked, head tilting down and into Darian's line of sight. "Putting it together now?"

Darian squirmed back, anger and betrayal in his eyes. "Y – ... we c-alled a truce – !"

Calyx laughed, pressing a kiss to Darian's forehead. "You're adorable." Before Darian could try to bite or headbutt or kick them off, Calyx slipped off his lap, scooping up the mask from the back of the couch. "No offense, but I can't exactly have the FBI knowing where I live. Aaaaaaand you didn't tell anyone when you figured it out. That's on *you*, sweetheart. If you're gonna be that stupid, I can't help but take advantage." The gloves slipped onto their hands next. One by one, pieces of 'Show' covering up the 'Calyx' he'd met.

Darian stared desperately at them, still rolling his wrists and shoulders to try to get out. "Come on – come *on* – I – I fuckin' saved your ass! You could be in prison right now – !"

Show picked up a wad of black fabric, rolling it up and wandering closer. "Open up~"

Darian's jaw set, fear clear in his eyes as he stared desperately up at Show. " ... *Please*."

Calyx rolled their eyes, grabbing Darian by the jaw and *s q u e e z i n g* until his cheeks were cutting against his own teeth. With a choked grunt, his jaw slotted open – quickly pried open further by the thick black cloth that was stuffed between his teeth.

"I like you. I do." Duct tape shredded away and smoothed over his mouth before Darian could get anywhere trying to work the gag out again. "I just need you to be less ... unpredictable. You get that, right?" The grip on his jaw tipped his face up to stare at Show.

Defiance, anger, and fear all pressed hot and wet at the corners of Darian's eyes in response.

"I don't *want* to do this, you know. As pretty as you'll bleed, I'd prefer you whole." Show sighed, fingers tightening as Darian tried to wrench himself from their grip. "This is best for both of us."

Before Darian really realized what was happening, Show's masked lips pressed to his through the duct tape, fingers keeping him exactly in place, just in case the shock of that moment wasn't enough.

It was.

Eyes still open and staring into the black void that lingered in the holes of Calyx's mask.

When they pulled back, Darian had stopped struggling. Just ... staring.

A gloved hand ran through his hair, and Show stepped away. Stretching for a moment before they picked up their knife. "Make some pretty sounds for me, and I'll go easy on you. How's that~?"

Darian barely had a chance to grunt in response before Show's fingers pressed at the camera.

The light turned red.

For a few long seconds, Darian lived in suspended disbelief. Denial, really.

That Calyx wouldn't do this to him.

That, even though they'd just met or *whatever* (*shut the* fuck UP *with your logic*), that Calyx wouldn't hurt him.

Just like how he couldn't hurt Calyx.

He barely shivered as the knife trailed over his collarbone, cool and crisp and scraping. He knew it wouldn't draw blood. He couldn't believe Calyx would do this to him. He *wouldn't*. This was a test. A ... prank. A –

Blood dribbled down his chest before he registered the pain.

Sharp. *Deep*. Prickling at the ripped edges of the gash.

And Darian believed.

***

Most of the next hour or so was a blur. It felt like months. It felt like minutes. It felt like it would never end.

Darian never realized just *how much* blood was in his body. Wouldn't it run out at some point?

It never seemed to.

With each cut and slice and gouge, more and more and more poured from him, coating his chest in streaks of crimson and soaking through his slacks. It dripped onto the floor until his bare toes were smeared with it. It soaked through the linen drape behind them.

Finally, he knew what it was like.

So many months of wondering what it would be like to be in that chair. And now he was there.

Darian screamed.

He screamed so *much* – he hadn't even known what his own screams could do. He never knew how they could sound. It didn't seem like his own voice. They crackled and snapped and clawed up his throat just to be devoured by the cloth that muffled them away.

The knife seemed to never stop moving. His only breaks from the onslaught were when Show stepped back to drag his blood over the white cloth.

It filled with red far too quickly. *Far* too quickly.

When that final moment came, he was so dizzy with blood loss and pain. He knew now how Show kept their victims awake. Out of sight of the camera, smelling salts, hidden in Show's sleeve, would press under his nose. Cubes of ice at the back of his neck made him arch and shudder, gasping back to clarity – but no one saw that.

It was just part of the show.

Part of the pain.

It kept him lucid enough to scream and thrash and beg word-lessly through the gag until that moment when Calyx finally stopped.

They stepped away, picking up something out of frame.

A garotte.

... Darian's favorite.

It looked like Calyx asked their questions with purpose, and Darian's head immediately hung in the exhausted regret that comes with having been so thoroughly played.

Calyx's fingers ghosted against his throat first – then the wire of the garotte.

A pause.

A moment of suspense to make this grand finale all the more dramatic for their audience.

Then Calyx's grip tightened. Twisted.

The wire choked away his air. It pressed at his arteries immediately – each frantic heartbeat slamming uselessly against the wire.

Darian's exhausted, depleted body was thrashing again – newfound strength found in one final burst of adrenaline as he choked on tears and panic. On pain and air and nothingness.

Desperately trying to breathe. To stop the slamming in his head as his mind turned fuzzy.

He thought he'd break the chair with the force of his thrashing and flopping as the panic ripped through him, but the wood held strong. Calyx didn't relent.

He'd seen this before. Seen the wire saw through flesh and draw out blood. All but decapitating the victims. They'd choke on blood as it slid into their esophagus or gasping at nothing as oily slick slid down their neck.

His final thought before slipping into the darkness was a question.

... Why wasn't the garrote cutting him?

8

INTERMISSION

Pain.

Darian wished he could be cool and start off with a dramatic, badass-sounding intro line like 'He awoke to pain. An old, familiar friend.'

But they weren't old friends. They weren't friends at all, and it wasn't familiar.

It was just pain.

Air wheezed out of him as he processed the inferno that wrapped his body. Skin and flesh shredded from their places and screamed agonies at his blurred and distant mind.

He shifted a little, heart pounding against his skull as he registered just how thirsty he was.

"*Oh* – ! Hey, there you are. Thought I'd lost you or something."

... Not a welcome voice.

Darian grimaced, head rolling away from the sound – then wheezing as Calyx's weight shifted on the bed, disturbing the delicate balance of agony and consciousness.

"Awh, don't pull away from me – it's not like you can, anyway." A hand combed through Darian's hair. Calyx chimed a soft giggle, amused, as Darian's neck mindlessly stretched to chase that touch – the only sensation that wasn't bringing pain. "Awwww~ you're adorable."

Darian half-scowled, head turning away again as a kiss pressed to his nose.

"Come onnnnnnnnn~ I saved your life – aren't you at least a *little* grateful?"

Darian's throat was rasped with dehydration and unuse, but he crackled out the whisper, anyway. "*Y-ou ... y ou hhurt me –* "

Calyx snorted a laugh, ruffling Darian's hair. "I mean *duh*. What did you think I was gonna do? I'm gonna go ahead and blame the sheer patheticness of that sentence on the drugs, m'kay? No judgment from me, nope nope~"

Darian grimaced, eyes cracking open in a groggy scowl at Calyx. " ... *Wh' day's it?*"

Calyx checked their phone with a bright hum. "Thursday. You've been out for liiiiiiike thirty-something hours."

Darian's eyes strained down over his body. Covered in bandages and smelling like medicine. " ... *H-ow did y – ...* "

Calyx shrugged. "Patched you up enough you wouldn't die on me and gave you a blood transfusion. I avoided doing any major damage, so you should heal up in a couple weeks."

Darian frowned, looking over Calyx. " ... *Wh' ... are you doing – ?*"

Brow raise. " ... What, with you?"

... Small hum of confirmation.

Calyx shrugged. "Just keeping you, that's all. Obviously couldn't let you keep living, and ... wasn't ready to let you go. So." They took a moment to nitpick the way Darian's hair lay, brushing it from his brow. "Found a middle ground. You like it?"

Darian's face twitched away from Calyx. *"N-o, I don't ffuck-ing like this – "*

Calyx blinked a tight smile.

Then something cold and sharp pricked against Darian's aching throat.

"You sure you don't like this alternative? Because I can always skip back to plan A."

Darian froze, swallowing against the cool blade. " ... *I-ll ma nage – "*

"*Good~*" The knife pulled away, and a kiss pressed to his cheek.

Darian was quiet for a long few moments, just ... trying to focus on Calyx's fingers in his hair. " ... *Why d'you like me – ?*"

Calyx shrugged, fingers drifting down now to trace the lines of Darian's face. "You see me. You actually *appreciate* my work. Andddddddd I'm bored. Good enough answer for you?"

He did his best not to twitch under the little touches. " ... D*id ... y ... the video ... – "*

"Mm. Mhm. Sent it to your team. Saw on the news they think you're dead. There's like a candlelight vigil thing for you this Friday in the park. Isn't that sweet?"

Darian twitched a frown, eyes sliding away. " ... *S-ure.* "

"I'd totally go, but I feel like it'd be rude to leave you alone during your own not-funeral, y'know? We can have a movie night or something instead."

... Darian ... had no idea what to say to that. So, he said nothing at all. A small part of him was screaming for him to run. To lash out and hit Calyx. To sprint from the room or strangle them.

... The rest of him was too fucking tired to even get through considering that idea. He'd probably pass out if he tried to stand, anyway.

Aaaaaand Calyx was back to playing with his hair. No – braiding it now. Their little fingers were twisting it out as long as possible to tangle a small cornrow from the corner of his forehead. Keeping their hands busy, he supposed.

" ... C-an I ... get some water – ?"

"*Mm* – ! Right right right, you're probably dehydrated as fuck, one sec – " Calyx stood, crossing out of the room.

Darian stared after them, then finally let his eyes roam the space.

… Queen-sized bed. Not a spare room – this one was littered in things. Piles of clothes that weren't put away. A few articles that had missed the toss to the hamper. Pictures tacked on the wall. Pocket change and trinkets drizzled over the dresser. This was Calyx's room.

Whichhhhhh meant they probably slept next to Darian last night.

… And would continue to.

Greattttttt –

His eyes snapped back up to the doorframe as Calyx reentered, holding up a clear water bottle with a straw. "Got it – think you can sit up?"

Darian half-scowled at them, shifting up and shoving his elbows under his weight to scoot b –

Darkness.

Darkness and pain and delirium engulfed him for several long seconds, refusing to let him escape.

A voice cut through the fog, muffled and slurred.

Darian winced and twitched away from whatever was patting at his cheek.

"*There* you are." He could fucking *hear* the grin in Calyx's voice. "Guess the answer to that was 'no,' huh?"

Darian grimaced, head rolling away as the light finally returned to his world. *"A-ns'r to wha –* ?"

"Whether or not you can sit up." Something poked at his lips, drawing out a flinch. " ... It's just a straw, you're fine. It's water. Undrugged and everything."

Darian wanted so badly to give them some shit line like '*That's what you said last time*', but not only would that make Darian look even *dumber*, he had no choice here. His throat was practically sticking to itself with every swallow – he *needed* water and it wasn't going to come from anywhere else.

So. Reluctantly. He let his lips close around it, sucking down greedy mouthfuls of the fresh, cool liquid. A half-panic surged through his mind, mouth chasing the straw as it withdrew.

"Hey – chill out, there's gonna be more. You'll make yourself sick drinking it that fast."

Darian scowled, letting his head flop back against the pillow.

Calyx perched on the edge of the bed again after they set the bottle down. Their arm propped up on the other side of Darian, leaning over him. "Are you mad at me~?" Pouting.

Darian's head twisted further from them. *"N-o shit."*

Calyx cooed a sorrowful sound, fingertips ghosting over Darian's lips. "I'll make it up to you~! You'll see. You're going to *love* being mine."

9

DIRECTOR'S CUT

Darian eyed Calyx as they pushed into the bedroom. Smiling, as always. Not Darian, of course – Calyx. They were still in their leotard from rehearsal. The one they'd dyed with his blood.

Charming motherfucker.

"I got something for you~"

His suspicion just kept rising. How could it not? The past couple days with Calyx had been mind-achingly dull and filled with healing pains when his captor was out of the house. When they were there, Calyx's schedule for Darian had included cooing, coddling, and endless ramblings about films, dance rehearsal, or childhood pets.

It didn't make sense. Not really. Still, Darian was slightly eased somehow by the fact that Calyx had been truly as obsessed with him as he was with them all this time. Made him feel just a little bit more sane. At the very least, less alone in his insanity.

Calyx proudly held up a box. They looked like they might explode from excitement.

Darian raised a brow slightly, eyes dancing over the box. " ... Am I supposed to know what that is?" It had very little in the way of markings besides the standard delivery company logo.

"No! It's a *projector~*"

Darian forced his eyes away again. "Going to pacify me with T.V. shows while you're gone?"

"Nah, I can do better than that." They hopped onto the bed and plopped down cross-legged, opening the box and pulling out the miniature projector which they'd apparently already opened and assembled outside.

Darian watched quietly as they worked, disliking the way they loomed above him even at that distance. He was sick of having his hands tied above his head. He'd have to ask them to shift the restraints again soon, or his arms were going to lose blood flow. And heaven *forbid* they not get to see his muscles anymore. Yes, that *was* sarcasm.

Calyx actually shut up for once while they set the projector up. They just put it on the end table and pointed it at the ceiling before plugging the wires into their laptop.

Through all the clicking, tapping, shifting, and frame-adjusting, Darian couldn't help but let the question tumble from his mouth: "What are we watching?"

Calyx's grin split across their face, eyes still focused on their work – almost hiding from Darian. "Some home videos, that's all~"

Oh.

Oh, *shit.*

Darian started to protest only to have his objection cut off by an image of *himself* in the chair popping onto the ceiling. The words died in his throat as realization set in. Of course. Of *course* Calyx would make Darian watch *himself* get tortured. Why the fuck did he think it would be anyone else?

"I had to edit it a bit for the official release, but we can enjoy the director's cut~!" Calyx hit play and set the laptop aside, snuggling down on their back next to Darian to stare at the ceiling.

Darian's chest felt tight. It's always strange seeing yourself in a video. The way you speak. The way you hold yourself. The way you breathe or walk or smile. All the things that photographs don't show.

But this was different. More. It was surreal. His current body was in so very much pain, yet the body he saw on the ceiling was completely untouched. Yet, somehow, that Darian on the screen, who looked so much younger and stronger, seemed to know exactly where each drop of blood would fall. The phantom agony spun in his mind, creating an endless loop of agony and fear. His mind teased him with the memories of the nothingness interrupted by blinding pain, which ebbed away into this stitched and healing state. Then back to the start again, awaiting the blood and the occluded screams.

Darian's eyes closed, head twisting away from the display.

"*Awhhhh~* don't be like that. I made a movie of us together, don't you wanna see it?"

Darian's head twitched a shake. "*No.*"

Calyx sighed, snuggling in closer where Darian had tried to wriggle away from them. "Darian. Don't pretend you're better than this. You've already watched me kill and torture plenty of people. Are you *really* gonna get a weak stomach on me just because it's *you*? I'd have thought you were tougher than that … "

Darian's jaw set, head turning to glare nose-to-nose at Calyx. "I don't *want* to watch you hurt me. I don't *want* to watch you hurt *anyone*."

Calyx moved slowly. Their eyes lost that smile, but kept the sparkle somehow, as delicate fingers moved up to brush Darian's hair away from his brow. "*You don't need to lie to me, Darian.*"

His stomach twisted.

They couldn't know. They could *not* – they were just conceited and brash.

Calyx's fingers ghosted down his cheekbone. "*I've watched you. Watched you watching me. I know you like it. I know this is the only video you won't have memorized by now.*"

Dread and panic tangled for dominance in his gut, and he twisted his head to glare at the opposite wall. "I'm n – "

A bruising grip cut off his thought as Calyx's fingers snapped his head back toward them like a vise around his jaw. "Do **not** lie to me." The grip relaxed slightly. "You don't have to. Not to me. To everyone else, yes – but not to me. It's okay to like it. It's done. Might as well enjoy it."

The urge to fight them was so incredibly strong – a strength much better suited to the Darian projected on the ceiling. *This* Darian, however, was bleeding, broken, and rotting tied to a bed. This man didn't have the strength to fight the accusations. Couldn't think of a lie any more easily than he could wrench his face from his villain's grip.

"*It's okay,*" they murmured, grip softening to cradle his cheek. "*It's just me. No one to impress.*"

Darian's jaw twitched, but he let his eyes slide to the ceiling. Ignoring the strain that put on his headache, he let his eyes linger over the shape of Calyx straddling his lap, tracing a knife over him just out of sight. But he could tell where it was. He could feel each millimeter of skin and scar pucker up around the invisible memory of the blade.

"*You're so fucked up,*" he murmured back, eyes still away from Calyx.

"*I know.*"

The video kept playing – getting now to the part that Calyx would have left in the 'final' edit. The silent strolling around the victim in the chair. Strolling around *him*.

"Gods, I *love* that expression you have. Defiant and angry but there's also sparks of passion? Stunning, really – soooo nice to look at."

Darian snapped a glare back to them, trying to burn a hole through their skull with his eyes.

They sputtered a bubbling laugh, sitting up a little and pointing at his face. "Yes! Yes, that one! Exactly!"

Anger and frustration were clawing up his neck now, bringing heat to his face and down his spine again. Darian snapped his eyes back to the 'screen', if only to avoid further scrutiny.

Calyx kept smiling over him, though, finger tracing the collar of his shirt. "Adorable," they chimed before settling back down next to him.

Darian trained his eyes on the 'home film' projected onto the smooth white ceiling, trying to maintain a blank expression to keep Calyx shut up.

He didn't notice before – maybe it was from the pain, abject horror, or belief that he was about to die, but ... Show treated him differently than the others.

It wasn't much. Small things. Things that no one but him would be able to pick up on. At least, he hoped no one would. He didn't need the entire BAU making fun of him when he finally got out of here.

But Show was ... sweet with him, almost. The cuts were precise and focused – made ever so slightly slower than usual. Like they were treasuring it. Their masked face was tilted up – watching his expressions through each moment, regardless of how small.

Even as Darian thrashed and screamed, gentle fingers smoothed his hair and traced the lines of his face. Not possessive, like they usually were with others. Just ... touching. Almost comforting. Tender.

Darian's breath was growing strained as he watched, noting how Calyx's fingers tended to drift – idly tracing sutured cuts with feather-light touches as Show created them on the screen. Reminiscing.

It felt ... surreal. Detached and separate. As if that wasn't *really* Darian on the screen. As if that wasn't Calyx.

This moment felt so much more real than that daze of a memory that Calyx committed to film. It was Agent Shah and Show on the screen – not Darian and Calyx.

That was easier. Easier to see Agent Shah bleeding and begging. Easier to see Show with fingers in his hair. It made him a little more certain that the Calyx next to him wasn't about to gut him again. Made it easier to believe that the gentle touches would stay gentle.

And they did.

Darian and Calyx both laid in silence for the hour or so that the film lasted, eyes locked on the screen as Show tore Shah apart.

When the film pulled to a stop, options to replay or rewind popping up on the ceiling, Darian's head fell to the side, face hiding against Calyx's hair. Even in calling them 'Shah' and

'Show', the threat still wriggled through. *I can do this again. Any time.*

He closed his eyes, buried in the surreal, yet gentle warmth of the moment. *"... Can you move my arms? I'd like to sleep."*

"Mm," they hummed back, turning to nuzzle against him in turn. *"Of course, baby."*

10

SHOWCASE

"Quit being such a *baby* – I could just stab through it again to cut them, would you rather I just do that?"

Darian grimaced, forcing his shuddering breaths still as he glared up at the ceiling. "... *N-o* – ?"

"Then hold still – ?" Calyx's little sewing scissors slipped under another stitch, snipping it free. They weren't exactly *gentle* with these blades. Calyx was like a swan gliding across a glassy lake when they had a knife in their hand. Yet, with dainty, inch-long silver blades from a delicate little sewing kit? Chainsaw fucking massacre.

Calyx kept going, rolling their eyes whenever Darian flinched or winced. "You're being *dramaticccccc*," they chimed, glancing up at Darian. They'd positioned themself between his legs, kneeling on the ground to get to the lower cuts without blocking the kitchen light.

Fuckin' classy.

"You're *cutting* me – !"

"I have, can, and *will* stab you if you don't hold the fuck still."

"You *ARE*." Stabbing him, that is.

"I'm barely pricking you – you aren't even bl – ... oh. Oh, you *are* bleeding. Huh~"

Darian groaned, head tipping back to glare at the ceiling again. This would be easier if Calyx would just let him take them out himself. Of course they wouldn't. They didn't trust Darian without his hands tied, much less with a sharp object in those untied hands.

His days with Calyx were simple. They'd fallen into a routine over these last few weeks. Darian stayed in bed, sleeping next to Calyx with hands bound to the fucking headboard. Moved for bathroom breaks. For meals. For movie nights with Calyx snuggled up against him or on his lap. Always fairly heavily bound, though Calyx was at least attentive enough to realize that Darian's arms had to be tied in different directions fairly regularly to keep up decent blood flow and mobility.

They were weirdly good about it.

Good about keeping his cuts and stab wounds cleaned. About checking the stitches. About massaging blood down his arms when they'd been tied in one place too long.

Right now, Darian was in a kitchen chair – hands bound individually to the cross of the chair legs and the bar that supported them. Still hurt.

"Can you j – *shhhit* – c-an you just fuckin' – *I* don't know, put on some glasses or something!?"

Calyx poked the little scissors up under Darian's chin, eyes glinting in amusement. "Maybe I just like how pretty you look covered in blood – ever think of that~?"

Darian scoffed a sigh, head rolling away from the scissors. "Just ... fuckin' ... hurry up."

Calyx laughed softly, hand dragging down Darian's chest. "But it's so *funnnnnn* – just look at all these marks. Some of my finest work, really."

Darian shivered as Calyx trailed the tip of the scissors over one of the freshly freed cuts. This one laid just below his ribcage on the left, following the long line of the prickling scar. "Everything was so well-balanced ... I made you so *pretty~*"

Darian's eyes roamed down, following the little silver points as they danced over his skin.

... Calyx was right.

He wasn't gonna fucking *say* that, of course. The bitch had too big a head already.

"Glad you're fuckin' satisfied."

Calyx leaned forward, tongue pressing to one of the marks – pricks of blood were beading up from where they'd pulled the sutures too roughly across the inside of his hip.

Darian's words choked to a stop in his throat as Calyx's tongue dragged up the mark – eyes locked on his. Blood gathered over their tongue, smearing over flesh as Darian squirmed back, eyes sliding away. That was a little close to the beltline, don't you think, Cal?

Calyx just smirked a bitten grin, moving back to their work. "Don't be so modest, Dari. You look *gorgeous~*"

Darian's skin twitched under the snips. At the sounds the little scissors made. At the way the stitches tugged at the inner lining of flesh. He was almost surprised when Calyx seemed to skip over one spot, but considering the gash across his side was giving him the most pain lately, he had to assume it was left intentionally. Larger wounds take longer to heal. Maybe the stitches weren't ready to come out yet on that one.

"Not even a 'thank you'?" Calyx's fingers drifted over his side, ticklish as they located the next spot to maul.

Darian's jaw tightened. "I don't need to *thank* you for anything. *You* did this to me. Giving me medical treatment is the absolute bare minimum you can do now."

Calyx chimed a laugh, stopping to look up at him from their spot between his thighs. "Not about the *stitches*, dummy! For the compliment!" Darian's eyes snapped back down as they kissed just above his navel. "Y'know? Because I think you're so pretty~?" They flutter-blinked up through their lashes at him.

Muscles and skin tightened under the touch, expecting the pain that Calyx's touches so often brought.

None came. It was just a kiss.

Darian's jaw tightened and untightened several times, assessing.

They were fucking with him. They always were.

He moved his eyes away again, roaming the kitchen counter and its crumb-spewing toaster. "I don't care if you think I'm pretty."

Calyx pouted up at him. "No? I'd have thought you'd want to know if the feeling was mutual."

He –

How was he supposed to respond to that? Agree? Say Calyx *wasn't* pretty? That would be a flat-out lie, and Calyx wasn't stupid.

Evasion, then – "You can't read minds, Cal. You don't know what I think."

"Hmm ... don't I~?"

Darian was *going* to snap at them, but a sharp breath punching down his throat cut that off as Calyx's hand drifted between his legs and cupped the bulge of traitorous flesh under his pants.

So much more sensitive than he realized. And *annoyingly* hard. The motherfucker.

Darian's jaw set, trying not to move. Moving would just come off as grinding. Like he wanted this.

He definitely didn't want this.

"You're such a fucking creep," he muttered, eyes as neutral as possible as he attempted to focus on the wall.

"You think I'm cute. Admit it~"

Darian couldn't help but squirm a little against the ropes as that hand palmed down and back up again, sending shivers of pain-pricked pleasure up his spine.

"I'm n – you can't j – ... Calyx, *stop.*"

They gave a contemplative hum, now stroking him in earnest through the fabric. It was so fucking annoying how good that felt. "I'd stop if you weren't hard, sweetheart. *You* started this. *Not* me."

Darian shifted again as fabric tugged down, cool air brushing over sensitive skin.

Then warm lips.

He tried to shove at them with his leg, but that just ground him against them more, earning a warm, tickling chuckle over his cock as they kissed down it. "No point in fighting it – and I'm getting *tired* of pretending we don't like each other. Aren't you?"

There was probably a good response to that. A proper response. Something that wasn't abject, knee-jerk denial. If that clever response was out there somewhere, it was washed away in the sensation of Calyx's lips closing around his head, tongue twirling slowly around it.

And Darian didn't have the brains to lie. He just didn't.

So much of his energy was taken up by healing lately, and being a defiant little shit was running him ragged. Exhaustion ate through his bones quicker than termites chewed through a pine foundation. Even before that, Darian was so damn tired. In life. In work. In the gasping in-betweens that he'd spent inhaling every scrap of Calyx he could find.

He didn't have the strength to lie anymore. The most he could manage was closing his eyes to pull them away from Calyx's smug gaze as he ground further into their mouth and the warm, intoxicating bliss it would bring.

11

THE SHOW MUST GO ON

Finally.

Fucking *finally*.

After weeks of working and trying and stretching, he'd finally managed to slip his thumb from the ropes that kept his wrists locked against the headboard.

Darian's eyes slid to the side – to Calyx's softly snoring form curled up next to him.

Then to the clock. It was late – 3:32. Calyx should stay knocked out for hours.

He'd have plenty of time to run and actually get out. Get help.

Carefully, he inched numb, aching limbs through the knotwork until one hand slipped from the bonds – eyes on Calyx the entire time.

Then the other hand – far more easily that time without the tension from the first.

His shoulders screamed in protest as they always did, creaking as he rolled them forward, finger circling his wrists to knead away the burn and pull the ropes left in his raw skin.

... He lay there. Thinking. Watching Calyx sleep.

Their breath puffed out softly, each press of air pushing a soft, honey-colored curl from their lips, then letting it fall back again.

... He eyed the door.

The clock.

... That curl.

... Aching, but gentle, fingers picked it up, brushing it away so it wouldn't tickle Calyx's nose anymore while they were trying to sleep.

He breathed in that tranquility for a moment. Then moved in a flash.

He straddled Calyx, pinning them down with a hand to their throat – the other snatching a wrist that immediately shot up to try to push him off. He pinned that to the mattress beside their head, looming over them.

Calyx's eyes were wild, disoriented, and – for the first time Darian had ever seen – fearful.

They shared panting, strained breaths before Darian's fingers started constricting, cutting off Calyx's air – past the wheezing chokes and into the silent hiss of thrashing that Calyx quickly stilled.

Darian's eyes narrowed, eyes roaming over his captor's face. " ... *Stop fuckin' snoring*."

Calyx stared up at him, then – slowly – nodded, fingers rippling around his wrist.

" ... *Thank you*." His fingers unwound from Calyx's throat, and he shoved off of them, flopping back onto his side of the bed. He laid on his side, curling away from Calyx. Glaring at the wall. Wondering why he was still there.

He listened to Calyx sputter a few ragged coughs as they massaged their throat, pulling down fresh air.

An arm slipped around Darian's waist. He did nothing to shove it off.

A grin pressed against his back. He continued to glare.

Calyx pulled in a breath to speak.

"Shut **up,**" Darian interrupted before they could even begin.

Calyx did, nose nuzzling into his back as they curled in close.

Calyx didn't tie him up anymore after that night.

12

CAMERA SHY

There was a clothesline outside the house. A small thing, really. Just big enough to hold one load of laundry, then you'd need to stop for the day and wait for the clothes to dry. Calyx used that little thing to hang the blood-soaked linen for days, ensuring the rusty hue was fully sun-baked into the fibers. Then they'd soak and hand-wash it with cold water in a large basin before hanging it out to dry again. Only in the final wash would they add detergent, and then hang it out for one final bask in the warm light of day.

Even if Calyx didn't treat their victims well, their blood was precious to them. It was precious to Darian now too. The transformation from human soul to stunning custom clothing was a simple but delicate one, matched with every ounce of tender care Darian and Calyx could manage.

When Calyx was gone at a performance or rehearsal, Darian occupied himself with several different, though equally monotonous, tasks throughout each day. He cleaned, cooked, did puzzles or read, but his favorite thing to do was to go through all of Calyx's uncut videos that they had lying around. He'd seen many of them dozens of times already, but these were the originals. Prime and perfect. Completely untouched by editing programs and the horrid cropping and trimming tools.

Of course, Calyx found this adorable. They seemed to find everything Darian did adorable, but Darian wasn't about to complain about that. Not anymore. It was endearing, in a way. He had always been too much of something or other to be properly 'adorable'. Too tall. Too masculine. Too annoying. Too muscled. Yet, Calyx called him 'cute' without even a hint of that sarcastic, condescending tone.

Alright, maybe there was *some* condescension there, but Darian knew that was flirtation, so Calyx got a pass and got to keep their perfect little nose unbroken.

Calyx had finally gotten some Corona in the house for him as well. They even kept limes stocked in the basket on the kitchen counter at all times, and Darian cut them into chunky half-slices in his free time so he could have one with each bottle as God intended. It was another long and slow day with cold beer in hand and feet kicked up on the ottoman as Calyx's car crunched over gravel, a cacophony of distant chaos announcing the arrival of his fair nemesis. Darian didn't get up or react, he just kept watching the clip he was analyzing. His favorite one. The one with the garotte at the end.

He had wondered so often before any of this if Calyx told their victims what was going to happen in that chair. Whether they knew if the film would be sent to their soon-to-be-thoroughly-traumatized families.

They did, surprisingly. At the beginning of each movie, there was an added clip of Calyx explaining it all in sweet, simple terms.

"You're going to die within the hour."

Cue pleading and crying or fighting or begging or whatever the whelp in the chair was inclined toward.

"There's no stopping it. I'm going to mutilate you on camera, then I'm going to send the video to your family. They'll probably report it to the police, but they won't catch me. I've done this a lot, and no one has yet. Feel free to be angry or hope that I'll be killed if it gets you through this better. Maybe you can even cry out some clues for the camera, yeah~? Just scream nice and loud for me, won't you? Give it a try~"

Darian caught himself smirking at that as the bottle pressed to his lips again and the bubbling bright amber washed over his tongue. Calyx had quite a way with words. A way that usually made Darian want to cut their tongue out, but still, they made him smile too much. So, the tongue and the words stayed.

Darian's eyes drifted over the fabric on the line outside. This one wasn't from the video he was currently watching, obviously – this fabric was from some other poor fuck last night. Still, they looked much the same. Soaked almost completely in red.

This particular batch was headed for its first round of washing. Soon, the thick, crusted chunks of blood would be flushed away, leaving a delicate hue on soft fabric.

Darian's eyes pulled to that piece – even away from the film he was watching. It danced and spun in the breeze, wrapping and twisting in an intricate, timeless dance. It reminded him so much of how Calyx moved. How they spoke. How every breath they took was like magic, flowing in and out of them in a languid yet bright refrain.

Calyx's key scraped into the lock, dully ringing through the house.

Darian skipped ahead through the film a bit, rewatching a part that caught his eye on the last two playthroughs. He spent the long moments of waiting by analyzing the way Calyx's gloved fingertips tilted their captive's chin up to get better access to the throat.

Most people would fight that or, trembling, twitch upward. Obedient yet fearful. Instincts thrashing against each other in a torrential battle. This time, however, their head lifted, hinging on their spine like a flower opening to the morning sun. Almost like they wanted it. Like it was a dance. As if this moment could hang in eternity flawlessly, without wither or waste.

Maybe she'd simply responded to Calyx's movements in kind, matching pace and matching tempo with her torturer as if that would save her. Maybe with someone else, it would have.

Calyx hacked off his train of thought as they finally stepped through the garage door into the kitchen, keys dropping onto the side table. "Backkkk~" they chimed, shoes fumbling against the ground as they kicked them off and fabric rustling as they slipped off their jacket.

Darian lifted his beer so Calyx would see him over the back of the couch, regardless of how much he'd slouched. They'd probably be able to realize easily enough that he was there just because the T.V. was on, but he didn't want to leave Calyx unanswered.

Silent footsteps brought Calyx's fingertips to Darian's shoulders, massaging there for a moment before sliding down his chest and twining together in a lazy, half-backward hug. They kissed his cheek from their perch behind the couch. *"Miss me~?"*

Darian lifted a hand, fingers threading through the curls even as he kept his eyes on the TV. "How was rehearsal?"

Calyx shrugged, unwinding enough to kick a leg over the back of the couch and slide down next to Darian. "It was fine. Jen still can't fucking count, but what else is new?" They swung one leg over Darian's, nestling in properly.

"I made muffins."

Calyx perked up, twisting to see back into the kitchen. "What kind – ? Where?"

Darian rolled his eyes, setting down his beer. "Blueberry lemon. Want one now?"

"Fuckkk – yes please, I'm dying over here."

Darian pushed himself up to standing and wandered back into the kitchen, not bothering to stop the little home film from playing. It was good sounds. Good screams. He opened the little tin he'd stored the muffins in and plucked one out. "Get the body sorted?"

Calyx shrugged, arms crossing over the back of the couch with chin resting on their arms. "Sure, it's not rocket science."

"Y'know, I could help out sometimes."

Calyx scoffed, hand held out for the muffin as he approached again. "*Could* you? Maybe in a few months, sure, but you'll tear stuff back open if you try to lift a *body* right now, Dari."

The muffin plonked into their palm, and Darian leaned on the back of the couch. "Maybe, but I still wanna help."

Calyx grinned up at him even as their fingers plucked the paper lining away from the treat. "What, you wanna do the next one~?"

Fuck their little smirky face.

"No."

"*Awhh*, why not~?" Their cooing would normally keep trilling a beat or two, but it was quickly cut short by a thick mouthful.

"I'm not going to *kill* someone, Cal."

"*Bhy noph* – ?" There was a literal, audible *gulp* as they swallowed that down.

"Because that's ... bad?"

Calyx puffed a laugh, losing a few crumbs from between their lips. "What – ? And it's just ~*fine*~ to watch me, but if you gotta hold the knife, that's different somehow?" They chomped into the muffin again.

" ... Yes."

"*Is'not diffren',*" they assured at a muffled mumble, shoving the last of the treat into their mouth. Evidently they *were* hungry, damn. He'd have to get started on supper soon.

"It's different, yes. It's more active."

Calyx finally took a moment to chew before responding, finger held up to indicate he was to wait patiently. "*Ehhh –* legally, no, though?"

" ... Well, I feel better about watching. And I don't like being on camera."

Calyx raised a brow, crumpling up the paper liner between nimble fingers. " ... Are you ... *camera shy*?" They gasped at uncovering this great scandal.

Darian rolled his eyes, heading back toward the kitchen. "Sure. Fine. Yes. I don't like them. Don't like having an audience."

Calyx was silent in response. Which never happened. Ever.

Darian turned a wary squint back toward Calyx just to find the fucker holding up their phone, filming or photographing him – he didn't know which.

Darian's hand flew up to block the camera. "Hey – *hey* – !"

Calyx twinkled a laugh, arching and stretching to change the angle again and again as he tried to block it. "I'm helping~! Face your fear, darling!"

Darian's jaw set, and he returned to his work, hoping Calyx would get bored of this prank and drop it.

Calyx ... did not do that. What they *did* do was slip off the couch, still grinning as they danced closer, phone still pointed at Darian. They put on their most dramatic newscaster voice. "Alright, we're here ~*live*~ with Agent Darian Oslo Shah~! Agent, would you care to tell us how you make your muffins so delicious~!? What's your secret!?"

Darian couldn't help but laugh even as he tried to swat the phone out of his face. "Sto-*stop*! I'm trying t – What if someone *actually* sees that, huh? What then?"

"I'm sorry, Agent, this interview is *exclusively* about muffins! How do you get those little pieces of sugar on top so crunchy and perfect!?" Calyx was moving around him with phone held up dramatically – a wooden spoon which they'd pulled from the counter was now pointed at his face like a microphone.

Darian snatched for the camera.

Calyx pulled back just in time. "Nope – ! Gotta be quicker than that~!"

He tried again. Missing again.

Calyx was laughing so broad and bright that Darian couldn't help but laugh along, even as he lunged for them. They took off and Darian gave chase down the hall until he managed to catch their elbow.

He might have been injured, but he was still able to easily pin them against the wall, one hand on their throat to keep them there as the other wrenched the phone from their grip and tossed it harmlessly to the shag carpet.

Calyx grinned up at him, fingers gripping his wrist. "That was a very expensive camera, you know. News anchors spend thousan*ds of do – d – d –* " Their voice crackled away and Darian's grip tightened.

Darian's breaths were a bit thick, coming faster than they should have from that small bit of exercise. If Calyx could speak right now, he was sure they'd make some comment about being '*breathtaking.*' Not that they'd be wrong.

Darian's fingers lifted, tracing the outline of Calyx's gaping lips. Calyx pulled a softer smile from him by pressing a kiss to those fingers and tugging him closer, evidently not caring if Darian strangled them.

Ten feet away, the gasps, muffled screams, and pleas turned into a soft gargling frenzy as the Calyx on screen began to strangle their victim. Calyx's throat rippled under his fingers, laughter at the irony caught by Darian's grip.

Irony, sure. Or planning. Either way.

Darian dipped, chokehold loosening a bit as his lips melted over theirs. He dragged them closer with a hand on the small of their back, arching them into him so he could feel every delicious inch of them pressed close.

Calyx may have kidnapped him, but they were *his* now.

13

SHOWTIME

Calyx thought it was cute that Darian called them their 'murder clothes.' They thought it was even cuter when Darian was wearing them.

It was practical, really. The *vast* majority of the oversized clothes Calyx had were their 'murder clothes.' Hoodies and sweatshirts and oversized black jeans that they'd layer up when they were getting a little bloody.

Conveniently, those were the only clothes that fit Darian.

Not that he minded too much – the ever-so-faint stains across them were invisible to the naked eye, but Darian's fingertips could detect the faint traces of texture differences along the edges of each mark.

He didn't want to admit that wearing those bloodstains sent a small shivering thrill up his spine. He didn't mention it.

Calyx knew, though.

Darian saw how Calyx's eyes lingered on Darian's fingertips whenever he got caught tracing the outlines of the stains over his own chest or thigh or forearm.

Calyx didn't miss much.

They just gave him a little smirk and continued what they were doing. Sewing, most often. If they weren't taking care of their little house or off at rehearsal or a performance, they were making new practice outfits. Leotards and skirts and loose, off-shoulder shirts to wear over leggings.

Always of the same material. Rusted linen.

Of course, only Darian knew it wasn't normal ink that dyed those clothes. Only Darian saw just how much Calyx treasured that process of converting a blood-clotted mess into stunning clothing. Only Darian saw the gentle time and care Calyx put into washing the linen properly – *ensuring* that those bloodstains stayed right where they were.

Calyx liked wearing the blood.

More and more and more, the two were growing alike over Darian's time with Calyx.

Darian hadn't cut his hair in a month now. It was getting shaggy – curling at the tips. One day, Calyx had caught Darian with a pair of scissors, wet-combing it out in front of the bathroom mirror to try to trim it himself.

Calyx just wandered in behind him, hand splaying up the back of his neck and twirling around the little curls that tangled between their fingers.

"*I like it like this*," they'd murmured, pressing a kiss to the side of Darian's neck.

... And ... Darian put down the scissors. Without a second thought.

His hair wasn't as long as Calyx's by any means, but it was curling all the same. Calyx's hair. Calyx's clothes. Calyx's food. Calyx's bed.

Darian didn't know why he was surprised when Calyx handed him the mask.

Darian stared at it, that moment seeming to linger on and on forever.

Glancing to the captive as she struggled in the chair. As the tears streaked down her cheeks and soaked into the gag. Pristine, white linen hanging behind her. Framing the video.

Ready for blood.

And Darian just ... stared.

Calyx took Darian's hand, pressing the mask into it. "You can do this. You *deserve* this."

Darian blinked as his fingers curled around the edges of the plastic.

... He was dressed exactly as he should be. Head to toe in black. Exactly the size and shape Calyx took on-screen in all their layers.

The only thing missing was the gloves. And the mask.

He turned it over in his hands, letting the hollow black eyes bore into his own.

" ... *Cal* ... -"

"You can do this," they insisted, stepping back. They picked up the knife, offering it to him as well. *"I want to see you."*

Darian found his eyes back on the woman – Mari, her name was.

He ignored her desperate, muffled pleas, letting them fade into the background. His eyes were on Calyx again. Just them. Just now.

"... I ... I like to watch – "

Calyx shook their head. "You've watched enough. It's your turn to shine."

" ... What about you?"

Calyx rolled their eyes, heading for the camera. Adjusting the exposure settings. "I'll get the next one. We can do an every-other thing."

Darian's heart was slamming against his chest as he rubbed the edges of the mask.

No.

No, he couldn't do it.

He couldn't just ... become this.

Watching was one thing. Partaking was another.

" ... Okay," he murmured, turning the knife in his hand. Slipping on the gloves. The mask. Pulling up the hood.

Calyx glanced back at him with a fond smirk on their lips. "Good boyyyyyy~" they teased, rolling the settings to record.

Darian stepped up behind them, both arms snuggling around Calyx's waist. He let the knife prick against their ribs.

Calyx flickered, but breathed a soft laugh, head lolling back onto his shoulder. "*You're adorable.*" They twisted, pressing a kiss to Darian's cheek.

… He hated that he couldn't feel their lips through the plastic.

That was his last thought as his attention pulled back to Mari. His arms slipped away from Calyx.

He waited until the little recording light flickered red before stepping into frame.

14

ROLL CREDITS

Darian thought about leaving. He could do it any time he wanted. Sure, Darian himself would go to prison, but Calyx would be locked away and people would be safe.

And wasn't that his life's calling? To keep people safe?

This world is full of so much chaos. Life has a way of beating you when you're down and pinning you to the ground well before your grave is fully dug or ready. For so long, Darian wanted to control the chaos. To help track it down and smother it to death with paperwork, dedication, and brainpower.

Thing is, there was always so much left to chase. So many rumors and so many stories. There would always be another villain. There would always be murders and snuff films and atrocities. The darkness would come and come and come until it snuffed out what remaining sparks of life are left in this rotting world.

But no matter how much darkness came, Calyx would be there. Darian could be cliché and say they were the light that drove out the darkness; in reality, Calyx was only ever a speck of dark themself. Just another cog in the machine that was driving everyone to madness.

But at least as this world rotted away, Darian would have someone by his side, watching it all burn down alongside him. Laughing with him. Pointing out the blinded idiots stumbling and falling as they tried to outrun death.

Calyx made this world seem a little more doable. A little more right, somehow. Like the veil had been lifted and he could see everything for all its blunt, beautiful glory.

Darian picked up the knife that night, and would gladly do the same again any time Calyx asked him to.

She'd screamed so much.

Darian was glad Calyx took him up on the suggestion to add a mic dangling above the chair. It really made a difference in the playback.

As Darian and Calyx watched the film – tangled up in blankets on the couch with popcorn and beer that night – the sound was so much better than the ones before.

It was nice seeing it on a screen, too. Darian's old projector just didn't get the colors crisp enough. He wondered vaguely if that was his own fault – a flaw in his setup or too much light in the room. Or maybe it was just the projector itself that failed.

Maybe it was being able to feel Calyx's breath hitch as they watched that made it so much better. Feeling their muscles coil and tense at the best parts, relaxing into him again after that small burst of euphoria those moments left behind.

Calyx seemed to think Darian did well. When the film rolled to a stop at fifty-two minutes and thirty-one seconds, Calyx nuzzled into Darian's neck, kissing once.

Twice.

Their breath warmed across his skin through the whisper.

"*Again.*"

So Darian played it again.

ABOUT THE AUTHOR

Raised in the rural American midwest, Rae is a twenty-eight year old cat-obsessed gremlin who spends most of her time reading, writing, and gardening. She has been properly obsessed with writing since she wrote her first novel at fourteen, yet it took ten years after that for her to incorporate writing into her lifestyle and future goals. Her books and stories explore horror, dystopia, murder, and vouch for casual representation of LGBTQIA+ characters as a main goal and priority.

— • —

Before You Go

This is the seventh book in 12 Months of Whump, a series of whumpy novellas published by WPP throughout 2025. Each novella can be read as a standalone.
To stay up to date with the 12 Months of Whump series and other whumperfly-inducing projects, visit us at
https://thewhumpyprintingpress.tumblr.com/

www.ingramcontent.com/pod-product-compliance
Lightning Source LLC
Chambersburg PA
CBHW052014170626
46808CB00007B/2931